Ernie and His Merry Monsters

and Other Good-Night Stories

Ernie and His Merry Monsters

and Other Good-Night Stories

By Michaela Muntean
Illustrated by Tom Leigh

A SESAME STREET / GOLDEN PRESS BOOK
Published by Western Publishing Company, Inc.,
in conjunction with Children's Television Workshop.

ERNIE AND HIS MERRY MONSTERS

"That Robin Hood was a great guy," Ernie said to himself. "He and his merry men must have had a wonderful time living in Sherwood Forest and doing good deeds."

Ernie leaned back against a tree trunk. "Those were the days," he thought. "Sometimes I think we could use a hero like Robin Hood on Sesame Street."

Ernie closed his storybook and then he closed his eyes. Soon he was asleep, dreaming dreams of Robin Hood.

"Help! Someone help me, please," cried a little boy.

Luckily Robin Hood was nearby and heard the boy's cry. "What's the matter?" asked Robin Hood.

"My kitten, Fluffy, is in this tree, and he can't get down," said the boy.

"Don't worry," said Robin Hood. "I will blow my horn, and soon you'll have Fluffy back safe and sound."

The little boy stared at the figure dressed in green. "I've already tried calling and whistling," he said. "I don't think blowing a horn is going to help."

"Just wait and see," said Robin Hood, and he blew three loud blasts on his horn.

A few moments later three monsters came running down the street.

"This is my band of merry monsters," Robin Hood explained to the boy. "Meet Friar Tuck, Little John, and Will Scarlet."

"Wow!" said the boy. "That must mean *you* are Robin Hood."

"At your service," Robin Hood said with a bow. "We travel far and wide, doing good deeds and other heroic stuff. But now to the job at hand! Give me a boost, merry monsters, and I will rescue Fluffy."

The boy watched as Robin Hood and his merry monsters got Fluffy down from the tree. Soon the kitten was snuggled safely in the boy's arms.

"Thank you," said the little boy. "You were so brave!"

"Bravery is our business," Robin Hood answered. Then he and his merry monsters set off down Sesame Street in search of other good deeds that needed doing.

They hadn't gone far when they noticed a lady pacing nervously up and down the sidewalk. She looked very worried.

"May we help you?" asked Robin Hood.

"I dropped my ring and it rolled down there," said the lady, pointing to a grate in the street. "I'm afraid I'll never get it back," she added sadly.

Robin Hood peered through the metal bars of the grate. Sure enough, deep in the hole below the grate was the lady's ring.

"My merry monsters and I will help you," Robin Hood said to the lady. Then he whispered something to Will Scarlet, and Will ran off. He returned a few minutes later carrying a fishing pole.

Robin Hood tied a small magnet to the end of the fishing line. Then he lowered it through the grate. It was not long before he was reeling in the line, the magnet, *and* the ring.

"Oh, thank you," said the lady when Robin Hood handed her the ring. "That was so clever of you!"

"Being clever is part of our job," said Robin Hood as he and his merry monsters took a deep bow.

Someone was crying. At first Ernie thought it was part of his dream, but when he opened his eyes, he knew it wasn't. A little girl really *was* crying, and Herry, Elmo, and Cookie Monster were telling her not to worry.

"What's wrong?" Ernie asked.

"I've lost my puppy," said the little girl.

"And we're going to help look for him," said Herry.

Ernie did what he thought Robin Hood would do. "Let's organize a search party," he said.

It took a lot of searching, but at last they spotted the puppy, who had fallen asleep beneath some bushes.

"Thank you for helping me," said the little girl.

"Being helpful is our business," Ernie said.

No one knew what he meant, but that didn't matter. Ernie knew. He knew there were times when a hero like Robin Hood was just what Sesame Street needed.

THE BIG BAD GROUCH

Oscar took a deep breath and blew as hard as he could. He took another breath, and then another, huffing and puffing over and over again.

Big Bird was on his way home, but he stopped to watch. He couldn't figure out what Oscar was doing, so he asked him.

"Can't you see I'm practicing?" said Oscar.

"Practicing what?" Big Bird asked.

"The Grouch Theater is putting on *The Big Bad Wolf,* and I'm going to try out for the leading role," Oscar explained. "I have to practice huffing and puffing and blowing down houses."

Big Bird scratched his head. "I thought that story was called *The Three Little Pigs,*" he said.

"Listen up, birdbrain," said Oscar. "I told you this is a grouch production."

"But you need the three pigs or you don't have a story," said Big Bird.

"Yeah, I know," Oscar admitted. "It's always a problem when we put on a play at the Grouch Theater. Every grouch wants the rottenest part—like the witch or the giant. This time everyone wants to play the wolf. No respectable grouch wants to play one of those silly pigs who built his house out of sticks or straw."

"The third little pig wasn't silly," said Big Bird. "He built his house out of bricks."

"That's true," said Oscar, "but the part of the wolf is the only part for me. Look, I've already made a poster." He held up a sheet of paper with his picture on it. Under the picture it read:

STARRING
OScaR THe GRoucH
AS
THe BiG Bad WoLF

"You've got to admit I make a wonderful wolf," he said.

"You were born for the part," Big Bird agreed. He was about to remind Oscar that the pigs catch the wolf at the end of the story when Oscar said, "You'd better beat it, feather face. I've got to get back to blowing practice. I don't want to *blow* my chances for the part. Heh-heh-heh. Get it?"

"I get it," said Big Bird. "And I hope you get the part, Oscar. A grouch like you deserves it!"

COOKIE CRUMBS

Elmo was on his way to do an errand for his mother. He had to buy some milk at Hooper's Store.

Before he left home, his mother had given him three oatmeal cookies. Elmo ate one of them right away and put the others in his pocket.

As he walked toward the store, Elmo thought about the story his
mother had read him the night before. It was called *Hansel and Gretel*.
Elmo thought it was clever of Hansel to leave a trail of breadcrumbs
so he could find his way home.

Elmo felt for the cookies in his pocket, and that gave him an
idea. "I know," he said. "I will pretend I am Hansel and leave a trail
of cookie crumbs. Then I'll follow them back home!"

Elmo broke off bits of the cookies and dropped them on the
sidewalk. He left a cookie trail to Hooper's Store.

After he bought the milk, he looked for the trail he had left, but
there wasn't one cookie crumb to be found.

When Elmo got home, he told his mother how he had pretended he was Hansel and had left a trail of cookie crumbs. "But the birds must have eaten them," he said.

From the window came a tweet, tweet sound. Elmo looked up to see Cookie Monster. He was flapping his arms and making sounds like a bird. Both Elmo and his mother laughed.

"It's lucky for me that I know my way home!" said Elmo.

"And it's lucky I have two more cookies," said Elmo's mother. "One for my little red monster—and one for this big blue 'bird'!"